JOHNNY THUMBS

written by Bob Hartman
pictures by Richard Max Kolding

STANDARD
PUBLISHING
Cincinnati, Ohio

The Standard Publishing Company, Cincinnati, Ohio
A division of Standex International Corporation
© 1993 by The Standard Publishing Company
All rights reserved.
Printed in the United States of America.
00 99 98 97 96 95 94 93   5 4 3 2 1

ISBN 0-7847-0093-1
Cataloging-in-Publication data available

Edited by Diane Stortz
Designed by Coleen Davis

CONTENTS

Chapter 1
THE KING WHO LOVED HOUSES

There once was a king

who loved fine houses.

One day the king said,

"We will have a contest.

The man who builds

the finest house

will marry the princess."

4

"What will happen
to the losers?"
asked the queen.

"We will chop off
their heads, of course,"
said the king.

5

Most men in the kingdom
wanted to keep their heads.
So only two men
entered the contest.
The first man
was Bill Builder.
"I will win the contest,"
he said.
"Then people will ask *me*
to build houses for them, too.
I will be rich and famous!
And I guess I will
have to marry the princess."

The second man

who entered the contest

was Johnny Thumbs.

Johnny could not

hammer a nail

without bashing a finger.

Johnny was "all thumbs."

That is how he got his name.

But Johnny loved the princess

with all his heart.

The king gave each man
land, bricks, and stones.

Bill Builder
picked up his tools
and started to work.

Johnny Thumbs picked up his tools

and looked at the princess.

He tripped

over a wheelbarrow

and fell flat on his face.

The contest had begun!

Chapter 2
BOASTS AND BUMPS

One week later,

the princess visited

Bill Builder and

Johnny Thumbs

to see how their houses

were coming along.

"See my straight walls,"

said Bill Builder.

"See my beautiful

window frames.

See how well

my door opens and closes.

No one can build

a house like me!"

"Your house is very nice,"

the princess said.

"But if you keep bragging,

you will get a big head."

Then the princess

went to see Johnny's house.

The walls were crooked.

The windows were cracked.

And Johnny Thumbs

was trying to put in

the door.

When Johnny

saw the princess,

he bowed.

When he bowed,

he dropped the door

on a stack of wood.

The wood

flipped into the air

and crashed into the wall.

The wall fell down

on top of Johnny Thumbs.

Johnny pulled a brick

out of his hat.

He shook cement dust

out of his ear.

"Thank you for coming,"
he said to the princess.
(But he wanted to say,
"You are wonderful.")

"I will come again,"
the princess said to Johnny.
(But she wanted to say,
"You are wonderful, too!")

Another week passed.

The princess visited

the builders again.

"See my tall roof,"

said Bill Builder.

"See my shiny floors.

See my smooth plaster.

No one can build

a house like me."

"You may be right,"

said the princess.

"But if you keep bragging,

you will get a big head."

Then the princess

went to see Johnny's house.

Johnny Thumbs

was working on the roof.

When he saw the princess,

he lost his balance

and fell off.

He knocked down his ladder.

He knocked down

bundles of sticks and straw.

Johnny pulled a ladder rung

out of his hat.

He shook bits of straw

out of his ear.

Then Johnny heard

the princess calling for help.

So he dug her out

from under a pile

of sticks and straw.

"I am so sorry," he said.

(But he wanted to say,

"You look beautiful.")

"That is all right,"

the princess answered.

(But she wanted to say,

"You are very kind

and brave.

Even if you are *very* clumsy.")

Chapter 3
A BIG HEAD

Another week went by.

The contest was over.

The king and the queen

and the princess

came to look at both houses.

One large soldier

with a very sharp axe came, too.

"Come in!"

called Bill Builder.

"Come into the finest house

in all the land!"

"See my beautiful furniture,"

Bill Builder said.

"See my fancy carpets

and lovely curtains."

"Ooh!" said the king.

"Aah!" said the queen.

30

"Pretty!" said the soldier

with the very sharp axe.

Bill Builder smiled.

No one could build

a house like him.

Just then there was

a puffing sound.

"Ooh!" said the princess.

"Aah!" said the soldier.

What are they oohing

and aahing about?

Bill Builder wondered.

I have not finished

telling them about my house.

Suddenly Bill Builder

felt his head

bump against the ceiling.

"I warned you

not to get

a big head,"

said the princess.

Bill Builder's head

crashed through the ceiling

into the second floor.

"Run!" shouted the king.

"Wait!" called Bill Builder.

"See my fine staircase!

See my strong chimney!"

The more Bill Builder bragged,

the bigger his head grew.

Soon his hair

touched the rafters.

Soon his ears

pressed against the walls.

"No one can build
a house like me!"
he yelled.

Then the house fell down
around him with a crash.

Chapter 4
THE HOUSE THE KING LOVED

"Bill Builder's house

was a fine house,"

said the king.

"But the princess cannot

live there now."

So the king and the queen

and the princess

and the soldier

went to see the house

that Johnny built.

When they arrived,
Johnny Thumbs bowed
and said, "Welcome."

But the king took one look

at Johnny's house and said,

"This house is not fit

for the princess, either."

The soldier with the axe

stepped forward.

"Please, father," said the princess.

"Give Johnny Thumbs a chance.

Just go inside."

So the king and queen

went inside.

"You are beautiful,"

Johnny whispered

to the princess.

"You are brave and kind,"

the princess whispered back.

"There *is* something special

about this house,"

said the king.

"What is it?"

"I love you,"

Johnny whispered

to the princess.

"I love you, too,"

the princess whispered back.

"That is it!"

shouted the king.

"This house was built with love!

Love makes this house

the finest house

in all my kingdom!"

Johnny Thumbs had won

the contest.

The next day,

Johnny and the princess

were married.

They moved into Johnny's house
and lived happily ever after.

As for Bill Builder,

the king could not find

an axe large enough

to chop off his head.

So Bill Builder wandered

around the kingdom.

"No one can build

a house like me!" he shouted.

And he is still looking

for a hat big enough

to cover his big head.